This
Nature Storybook
belongs to:

_____

_____

_____

WALKER BOOKS

About the author

When Vivian French's daughters were small,
they visited the pond next door each spring
to collect some frogspawn, bring it home and watch
the tadpoles hatch. (The cat was always
VERY interested.) Viv has written over 200 books
for children, including the Nature Storybooks
"T. Rex" (also illustrated by Alison Bartlett) and
"Caterpillar Butterfly" (illustrated by Charlotte Voake).
Her daughters are grown-up now
and she has moved to Edinburgh.

About the illustrator

Alison Bartlett's first picture book was
"Oliver's Vegetables" (also written by Vivian French)
which was recommended for the National Art Library
Illustration Awards. Before she painted the pictures
for this book, she thought frogspawn was "disgusting" –
now she thinks it's amazing! She lives in Bath
with her son, Joel, and their two Jack Russell terriers.

For Jane Slade
V.F.

For Rebecca, with much love
A.B.

Consultant: Martin Jenkins

First published 2000 by Walker Books Ltd
87 Vauxhall Walk, London SE11 5HJ

This edition published 2008

2 4 6 8 10 9 7 5 3 1

Printed in China

British Library Cataloguing in Publication Data:
a catalogue record for this book is available from the British Library

ISBN 978-1-4063-1206-5

www.walkerbooks.co.uk

Growing Frogs

Vivian French   illustrated by Alison Bartlett

WALKER BOOKS
AND SUBSIDIARIES
LONDON · BOSTON · SYDNEY · AUCKLAND

Once, when I was little, my mum read me a story about a frog that drank and drank and drank, and grew **bigger** and **bigger** and **bigger**.

Afterwards Mum asked me if I'd like to watch some real frogs growing.

"I know where there's a pond with lots of frogs' eggs in it," she said. "We could bring some home."

I was frightened. "I don't want any frogs jumping about getting bigger and bigger and bigger," I said.

But Mum gave me a hug. "It's only a story," she said. "Even when our frogs are grown up they'll still be smaller than my hand."

"Oh," I said. "OK."

Next day we went to look at the pond. The water was dark brown, and there was grey jelly stuff floating on the top.

"Yuck!" I said.

"There's the frogspawn," said Mum.
And she pointed to the grey jelly stuff.
"I bet that was laid last Friday night.
The frogs were croaking so loudly,
I couldn't get to sleep."

Male frogs croak to attract female frogs
for mating. The females lay eggs called frogspawn.

"You see the black dot in the
middle of each jelly shell?" said Mum.
"That's going to grow into a tadpole."

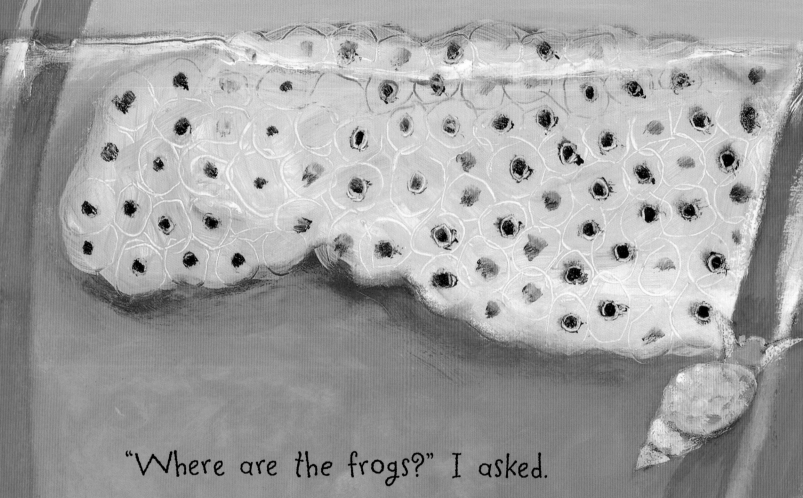

"Where are the frogs?" I asked.
"Tadpoles grow into frogs," she said.
"Little ones — no giant frogs here!"

Mum put some pondweed
and some stones into a bag.
She filled a bucket with
pond water, then I scooped
a *little* of the frogspawn
into it.

Always use pond water for growing frogs at home
Tap water has chemicals like fluoride in it,
which might poison them.

When we got home we put everything into a big fish tank in the kitchen.

The cat kept peering at it, so we had to put a wire net over the top.

12

I counted
twenty-seven
little black dots.
Each dot was inside
its own jelly shell.

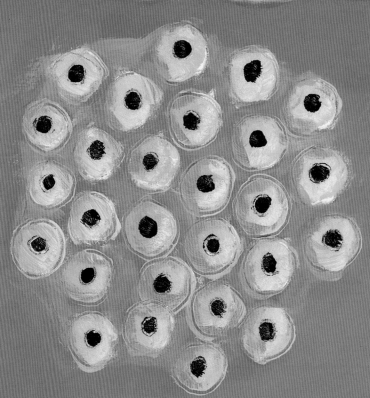

The tank needs to be somewhere that's
cool and away from direct sunlight.

13

Every day when I woke up
I went straight downstairs
to look at the frogspawn.

The little dots
grew into bigger dots,

and then into
tiny commas.

In a tank, the eggs hatch into tadpoles
about ten days after they are laid.

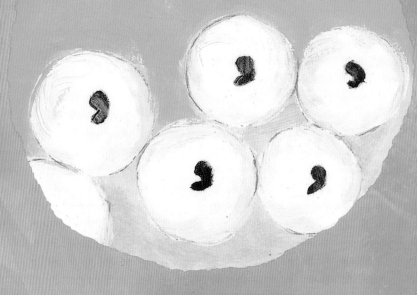

And one morning
I saw the first tadpole
wriggling out of its
jelly shell!

At first the tadpoles didn't do much.
They just stayed close to their jelly shells
and nibbled at the pondweed.

But after two or three days
they looked quite different. There
were feathery things on their heads
and I could see their eyes.

The feathery bits are called gills and they're
what underwater animals use for breathing.

They swam **very** fast.

Ten of the eggs
didn't hatch out.
The black dots went
dull and cloudy,
and Mum took
them away.

Then we cleaned out
the tank and put in fresh
weed and pond water.

One of the tadpoles swam
into my hand when I was
putting a stone back.
It was slippery and slithery,
and it made me jump.

After the tadpoles hatch,
the pond water needs
to be changed at least
twice a week.

After a bit I got used to having tadpoles
and I didn't look at them so often.
When Mum told me their little feathery bits
had gone I didn't believe her.

But it was true.

Tadpoles only have gills outside their bodies at first.
Then they grow gills inside their bodies
and the outside ones disappear.

It was me that saw the next change, though.

"Look!"

I shouted, and Mum rushed to see.
Some of the tadpoles had grown two
little bumps. Mum said the bumps
would grow into back legs.

They grew very quickly.

One day there were
two little bumps.

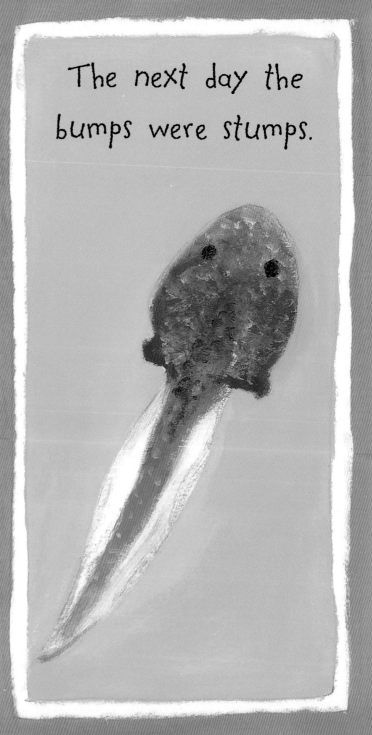

The next day the
bumps were stumps.

The day after that they were almost proper legs.

And when the feet unfolded they were webbed, like tiny browny-green fans.

"They aren't tadpoles any more," I said.
"They're not-quite-frogs."

The not-quite-frogs grew front legs next.

And then their tails got shorter

and their mouths got w i d e r.

"Now they're frogs," Mum said.
"Baby ones."

Soon the baby frogs were popping up and gulping at the surface of the water.

One of them tried to climb on to the stones, but it slid off. Mum said they were getting ready to leave the water.

"Grown-up frogs breathe air," she said. "That's what the stones are for — so our frogs can climb out of the water and breathe."

As tadpoles slowly turn into frogs, they grow lungs for breathing air and their gills disappear.

Not long after that Mum said it was time to take our baby frogs back to live in the pond with all the other baby frogs.

I was sorry to leave them, but Mum said we could come back and visit every day.

Baby frogs need space to grow and room to hop around. Grown-up frogs live most of their lives on land, only returning to their ponds to breed.

One rainy morning a week later
Mum woke me up very early.

"Hurry!" she said, and we ran downstairs
and out to the pond.

28

There were hundreds of tiny frogs hopping over the grass.

"They're looking for dark wet places to live in," Mum said. "But they won't go far, and in a couple of years they'll be back to lay frogspawn of their own."

"Will they be bigger then?" I asked.

"Just a little," said Mum.

"Good," I said. "I like having frogs jumping about getting bigger and bigger and bigger!"

Index

Look up the pages to find out about
all these froggy things.
Don't forget to look at both kinds of word —
this kind and this kind.

Frogs are in danger — please help!

Rules for frog-lovers

⊙ Don't ever take frogspawn from a wild pond.

⊙ If you take frogspawn from a garden pond, only take a LITTLE.

⊙ Always take your frogs back to the pond they came from.

Praise for Nature Storybooks...

"For the child who constantly asks How? Why?
and What For? this series is excellent."
The Sunday Express

"A boon to parents seeking non-fiction picture books to read
with their children. They have excellent texts
and a very high standard of illustration to go with them."
The Daily Telegraph

"As books to engage and delight children, they work superbly.
I would certainly want a set in any primary
classroom I was working in."
Times Educational Supplement

"Here are books that stand out from the crowd,
each one real and individual in its own right and
the whole lot as different from most other series non-fiction
as tasty Lancashire is from processed Cheddar."
Books for Keeps

Find notes for teachers about how to use Nature Storybooks in the classroom at
www.walkerbooks.co.uk

Nature Storybooks support KS 1-2 Science